THE USBORNE CHILDREN'S WORDFINDER

Anne Civardi

Illustrated by Colin King

Consultant: Betty Root
Series Editor: Heather Amery

With thanks to Lynn Bresler

KT-415-281

The building site

1 bulldozer
2 surveyor
3 theodolite
4 steamroller
5 architect
6 foreman
7 site hut
8 telephone bell
9 plans
10 ridge tile
11 profile board
12 workman
13 road drill
14 hardcore
15 loft window
16 tiler
17 roofing felt
18 batten
19 roof ladder
20 strut
21 rafter
22 ridge board
23 chimney stack
24 chimney pot
25 flashing
26 gable end
27 dump truck
28 cement mixer
29 cement
30 facia board
31 eaves
32 staircase
33 riser
34 tread
35 banisters
36 newel post
37 plywood
38 plasterer
39 float
40 plasterboard
41 straight edge
42 plaster
43 cavity wall
44 mortar
45 pulley
46 chipboard
47 shovel
48 bricks
49 floor joist
50 lintel
51 hacksaw
52 floorboards
53 ceiling joist
54 breeze block
55 plank
56 sill
57 electric drill
58 screed
59 wall tie
60 damp proof
    course
61 scaffolding

62 bricklayer
63 hod
64 trowel
65 T-square

4

66 bolster chisel
67 club hammer
68 hawk
69 plumb line
70 line and pins
71 brick hammer

72 spirit level
73 pointing knife
74 pickaxe
75 foundations
76 plumber
77 soldering iron
78 shave hook
79 adjustable
     spanner

80 file
81 wrench
82 blow lamp
83 cornice
84 window bars
85 radiator
86 electrician
87 electric wire
88 rungs

89 wire stripper
90 gutter
91 step ladder
92 burglar alarm
93 carpet layer
94 underfelt
95 tile cutter
96 floor tiles

97 roof insulation
98 light fitting
99 door frame
100 switch
101 ceiling
102 header tank
103 cold water tank
104 cold water pipe
105 hot water pipe
106 hot water tank
107 ventilation pipe
108 overflow pipe
109 timer
110 rainwater pipe
111 fuse box
112 gas boiler
113 gas meter
114 electricity
      meter
115 air extractor
116 waste pipe
117 gulley
118 stopcock
119 drainpipe
120 inspection pit
121 thermostat
122 socket
123 skirting board
124 linoleum
125 window frame
126 glazier
127 putty
128 latch
129 window pane
130 glass cutter
131 rubble
132 skip
133 tarmac
134 concrete
135 paving stones
136 carpenter
137 plane
138 hand saw
139 workbench
140 folding rule
141 chisel
142 hammer
143 awl
144 painter
145 paint
146 paintbrush
147 paint roller
148 paint tray
149 brace and bit
150 screwdriver
151 screws
152 mallet
153 nails
154 wallpaper
      glue
155 wallpaper
156 masking tape
157 wallpaper
      brush
158 sandpaper
159 stripping knife

The house

1 television aerial
2 roof
3 attic
4 boxes
5 cot
6 trunk
7 lampshade
8 lampstand
9 playpen
10 bulb
11 high chair
12 bedroom
13 curtain rail
14 striplight
15 mirror
16 father
17 wardrobe
18 curtain

19 headboard	25 shirt	31 cushion
20 sheet	26 duvet	32 chest of drawers
21 alarm clock	27 bedside table	**33 bathroom**
22 dressing table	28 blanket	34 airing
23 lamp	29 slippers	cupboard
24 pillow	30 bed	35 shower

36 towel ring	97 portrait
37 medicine	**98 hall**
cabinet	99 coat rack
38 toilet paper	100 telephone
39 towel	101 telephone
40 taps	directories
41 son	102 doormat
42 washbasin	**103 sitting room**
43 bath	104 bookcase
44 bathroom	105 photograph frame
scales	106 record deck
45 bathmat	107 stereo
46 lavatory	108 sofa
47 laundry basket	109 grandfather
48 vase	110 shelf
49 door	111 magazine rack
50 grandfather	112 window
clock	113 television
51 hamster	114 armchair
52 mother	115 coffee table
53 patchwork quilt	116 ashtray
54 vacuum	117 rug
cleaner	118 wastepaper
55 daughter	basket
56 rocking chair	119 toothbrush
57 bunkbeds	120 soap
58 fish tank	121 toothpaste
59 window box	122 bath salts
60 porch	123 cup
61 kitchen	124 saucer
62 chimes	125 comb
63 door bell	126 hair brush
64 cat flap	127 shampoo
65 bone	128 plate
66 dog bowl	129 soup bowl
67 tumble dryer	130 duster
68 bird cage	131 polish
69 kitchen cabinet	132 dustpan
70 worktop	133 scrubbing
71 sink	brush
72 blind	134 teapot
73 draining board	135 coffee pot
74 grandmother	136 washing
75 oven	powder
76 dishwasher	137 sugar bowl
77 tray	138 butter dish
78 washing	139 toaster
machine	140 tin opener
79 refrigerator	141 blender
80 freezer	142 knife
81 dresser	143 fork
82 fruit bowl	144 spoon
83 iron	145 toast rack
84 ironing board	146 carving knife
85 tablecloth	147 carving fork
86 table	148 corkscrew
87 stool	149 egg timer
88 bin	150 saucepan
89 bread board	151 frying pan
90 table mat	152 casserole dish
91 glass	153 ladle
92 napkin	154 salt-cellar
93 milk jug	155 peppermill
94 chair	156 candlestick
95 dog basket	157 colander
96 umbrella stand	158 kettle

Sports I

1 starting block
2 sprinter
3 track shoe
4 athlete
5 stadium
6 running track
7 arena
8 spectators
9 coach
10 marathon runner
11 starting gun
12 competitors
13 winner
14 finishing line
15 water jump
16 steeplechaser
17 hurdler
18 hurdle
19 long jump
20 high jump
21 crossbar
22 take-off board
23 triple jump
24 pole vault
25 race walker
26 javelin
27 discus thrower
28 shot put
29 safety cage
30 hammer thrower
31 relay race
32 baton
33 discs
34 barbell
35 weightlifter
36 wrestling boot
37 wrestler
38 contestant
39 flight
40 dart
41 darts player
42 scorer
43 scoreboard
44 dartboard
45 **karate**
46 high kick
47 karate suit
48 **judo**
49 black belt
50 judoka
51 **boxing**
52 headguard
53 boxer
54 referee
55 boxing ring
56 corner cushion
57 judge
58 time keeper
59 gong
60 manager
61 second
62 speedball

63 punchbag
64 punchball
65 dumb bell

66 **fencing**
67 fencing mask
68 fencing master

69 swordsman
70 half-jacket
71 breeches

72 foil
73 fencing glove
74 cuff

8

86 trampoline
87 rings
88 parallel bars
89 horizontal bar
90 pommel horse
91 instructor
92 wall bars
93 headstand
94 bench
95 landing mat
96 somersault
97 mattress
98 handstand
99 rope
100 golf
101 golf clubs
102 golf bag
103 teeing ground
104 golfer
105 golf trolley
106 caddie
107 tee
108 fairway
109 golf ball
110 putting green
111 flagstick
112 bunker
113 rough
114 club house
115 waterskier
116 waterskis
117 jumping ramp
118 tow rope
119 motor boat
120 tennis
121 umpire
122 linesman
123 tennis court
124 baseline
125 tramlines
126 doubles
    sideline
127 singles sideline
128 service line
129 tennis net
130 ballboy
131 server
132 tennis racket
133 grip
134 tennis ball
135 rollerskater
136 rollerskate
137 toe binding
138 toe stop
139 elbow pad
140 kick tail
141 knee pad
142 skateboard
143 high board
144 diver
145 swimming pool
146 diving board
147 lanes
148 backstroke
149 starter
150 bathing cap

75 épée	78 vaulting horse	81 beam	83 vaulting box
76 sabre	79 gymnasium	82 asymmetric	84 springboard
77 gymnast	80 leotard	bars	85 buck

9

Sports II

1 **skiing**	13 ski boot	24 **cricket**
2 ski jump	14 ski pole	25 fielder
3 mountain	15 **American**	26 batsman
4 cable car	**football**	27 cricket bat
5 chair lift	16 shoulder pad	28 wicket keeper
6 skier	17 thigh pad	29 cricket pad
7 piste	18 goal post	30 bowler
8 ski class	19 **soccer**	31 cricket ball
9 ski instructor	20 corner flag	32 stumps
10 toboggan	21 striker	33 bowling crease
11 slalom course	22 soccer ball	34 batting glove
12 ski	23 whistle	35 **rugby**

93 bowling mat	99 centre line	105 rifle range	111 squash court	117 bow
94 bowling green	**100 rifle shooting**	**106 boules**	112 squash ball	118 shaft
95 bowl	101 optical sight	107 boule	113 squash racket	119 arm bracer
96 jack	102 rifle	108 baguette	114 service box	120 target
97 table tennis	103 marksman	109 pitch	**115 archery**	121 bull's eye
98 table tennis bat	104 cartridges	**110 squash**	116 bowstring	**122 croquet**

10

36 scrum	48 base	59 racing colours	71 triple bar	82 brakeman
37 scrum half	49 pitcher's	60 racehorse	72 horse jump	83 captain
38 rugby ball	mound	61 whip	73 riding boot	84 two-man
39 lacrosse	50 pitcher	62 jockey	74 jodhpurs	bobsleigh
40 crosse	**51 ice hockey**	63 blinkers	75 riding hat	85 front runner
41 baseball	52 ice skate	64 winning post	**76 surfing**	**86 curling**
42 catcher	53 stick glove	**65 canoeing**	77 skeg	87 curling broom
43 baseball bat	54 goal pad	66 kayak	78 surfboard	88 skip (captain)
44 batter	55 goal line	67 bowman	79 surf leash	89 target circle
45 mitt	56 goal crease	68 deck	**80 bobsleigh**	90 rink
46 home plate	57 puck	**69 show jumping**	racing	91 curling stone
47 outfielder	**58 horse racing**	70 post-and-rails	81 rear runner	**92 bowls**

123 clips	129 polo stick	135 pelote (ball)	141 goal keeper	**147 rowing**
124 croquet mallet	130 polo pony	**136 basketball**	142 goal	148 skiff
125 hoop	131 ankle bandage	137 backboard	143 hockey stick	149 cox
126 croquet ball	**132 pelota**	138 basket rim	**144 badminton**	150 oar
127 winning peg	133 cesta (basket)	**139 hockey**	145 badminton racket	151 oarsman
128 polo	134 jai-alai (court)	140 faceguard	146 shuttlecock	152 boat house

On the farm

1 tools	16 mustard	31 lamb	46 mowing machine	61 water butt
2 hoe	17 kale	32 ewe	47 hen house	62 bird table
3 digging fork	18 sunflower	33 ram	48 feeder	63 wall
4 pitchfork	19 maize	34 boar	49 hare	64 hose
5 sickle	20 cob	35 snout	50 shed	65 kennel
6 potato rake	21 sugar beet	36 sow	51 hay net	66 puppies
7 hay rake	22 rape	37 piglet	52 stable	67 mud
8 scythe	23 clover	38 field	53 farmhouse	68 rabbit
9 spade	24 lucerne	39 shelter	54 shutter	69 rabbit hutch
10 blade	25 cow	40 paddock	55 kitten	70 farmer's wife
11 crops	26 udder	41 gate	56 cat	71 eggs
12 rye	27 calf	42 bees	57 pigsty	72 fence
13 wheat	28 tail	43 beehive	58 trough	73 reeds
14 barley	29 bull	44 tractor	59 besom	74 pond
15 oats	30 nose ring	45 hedge	60 boots	75 peacock

76 nanny goat	91 beak	106 sacks	121 milk tanker	136 roller
77 kid	92 hen	107 hedge cutter	122 milk	**137 farm machinery**
78 horn	93 scarecrow	108 farmer	123 dairy	138 forage
79 billy goat	94 furrows	109 corn	124 horse	harvester
80 mare	95 haystack	110 workshop	125 mane	139 combine
81 foal	96 silo	111 cowshed	126 saddle	harvester
82 donkey	97 shepherd	112 stall	127 rider	140 hay baler
83 duck	98 sheep dog	113 straw	128 reins	141 seed drill
84 duckling	99 sheep	114 hayloft	129 stirrup	142 cultivator
85 carthorse	100 weathervane	115 rat	130 hoof	143 harrow
86 turkey	101 sheep dip	116 ladder	131 fertilizer	144 plough
87 goose	102 fruit picker	117 barn owl	132 overall	145 manure
88 gosling	103 orchard	118 farm worker	133 dairyman	146 muck spreader
89 cockerel	104 cattle grid	119 farm manager	134 milking machine	147 hay elevator
90 feathers	105 barn	120 hay bale	135 trailer	148 potato harvester

At the airport

1 **instrument panel**
2 artificial horizon
3 airspeed indicator
4 altimeter
5 radio compass
6 boost gauge
7 tachometer
8 temperature gauge
9 turn indicator
10 control stick
11 throttle lever
12 rudder pedal
13 **light aircraft**
14 propeller blade
15 spinner
16 cockpit cover
17 aileron
18 landing flap
19 **helicopter**
20 tail skid
21 stabilizer
22 tail rotor
23 exhaust outlet
24 rotor hub
25 rotor blade
26 skid landing gear
27 **jump jet**
28 outrigger wheel
29 tail puffer
30 airbrake
31 fan air nozzle
32 pitot head
33 wheel well
34 **airship**
35 nose cone
36 gas bags
37 skycrane
38 **supersonic airliner**
39 droop nose
40 turbo-prop
41 executive jet
42 glider
43 **flying boat**
44 seawing
45 float
46 **freight plane**
47 hinged nose
48 **airport**
49 car park
50 radio aerial
51 floodlights
52 radar
53 control tower
54 ground control officer

55 flight plan
56 observation terrace
57 passenger bridge
58 cargo container
59 **jet plane**
60 elevator
61 tailcone
62 rudder
63 tail fin
64 national flag
65 tailplane
66 registration number
67 cargo hold
68 washroom
69 food trolley
70 bulkhead
71 emergency exit

14

72 reclining seats	76 spoiler	81 anti-collision	85 co-pilot	89 marshaller
73 cinema screen	77 wing tip	light	86 pilot	90 earmuffs
74 antenna	78 windsock	82 passenger cabin	87 flight deck	91 radome
75 supervisor's	79 runway lights	83 engine intake	88 airport police	92 nose wheels
van	80 runway	84 flight engineer	car	93 landing light

94 stewardess
95 fuselage
96 undercarriage
97 jet engine
98 engine cowling
99 maintenance
engineer
**100 passenger
terminal**
101 duty free shop
102 departure gate
103 security check
104 departure lounge
105 passport
106 airline ticket
107 boarding pass
108 hand luggage
109 flight indicator
board
110 conveyor belt
111 check-in desk
112 departure hall
113 flight
information
114 airport official
115 hotel
reservations
116 car hire
117 arrivals hall
118 customs
control
119 luggage
carousel
120 luggage
reclaim hall
121 immigration
officer
122 passport control
123 moving
walkway
124 airport vehicles
125 refueller
126 freshwater
tanker
127 air conditioning
vehicle
128 mobile generator
129 baggage train
130 snow blower
131 cherry picker
132 scissor-lift
transporter
133 lavatory
cleaning vehicle
134 crew bus
135 ice removal
vehicle
136 passenger
bus
137 tow truck
138 fire tender

The beach and the sea

1 cave
2 beach café
3 megaphone
4 telescope
5 lifeguard
6 changing room
7 ice cream stall
8 pedal boat
9 shrimper
10 bollard
11 lifebelt
12 promenade
13 windbreak
14 sun hat
15 umbrella
16 shrimping net
17 seal
18 seal pup
19 tideline
20 cormorant
21 swimming
   trunks
22 wing
23 beach bag
24 picnic hamper
25 beach towel
26 deckchair
27 sand
28 beachball
29 armband
30 cuttlefish bone
31 rock
32 bucket
33 sandcastle
34 spade
35 **rock pool**
36 razor shells
37 sea squirts
38 tower shell
39 oysters
40 claw
41 crab
42 sea anemone
43 Portuguese-
   man-of-war
44 sea lettuce
45 barnacle
46 mussels
47 whelk
48 cockles
49 limpets
50 goose barnacle
51 spider crab
52 shrimp
53 sea slug
54 periwinkle
55 egg case
56 sea urchin
57 hermit crab
58 starfish
59 scallop
60 lobster

61 pincer
62 jellyfish
63 dolphin

64 fin
65 seaweed
66 ray

67 eel
68 sailfish
69 spines

70 swordfish
71 octopus
72 siphon

16

85 lifeboat station
86 slipway
87 lighthouse
88 bay
89 island
90 raft
91 snorkel
92 fish boxes
93 net
94 frisbee
95 breakwater
96 windsurfer
97 swimmer
98 buoy
99 sea
100 flipper
101 goggles
102 seagull
103 surf
104 lugworm
105 anchor
106 crab pot
107 post
108 lobster pot
109 jetty
110 driftwood
111 wave
112 fisherman
113 fishing boat
114 pipefish
115 seahorse
116 turtle
117 sawfish
118 giant clam
119 porpoise
120 sea serpent
121 shark
122 whale
123 frogman
124 underwater
    camera
125 coral
126 mini submarine
127 conning tower
128 navigator
129 ballast tank
130 cage
131 cable
132 shipwreck
133 speargun
134 weight belt
135 aqualung
136 sea scooter
137 wetsuit
138 depth gauge
139 waterproof
    watch
140 oxygen tube
141 deep sea diver
142 diving helmet
143 trench
144 bathyscaphe
145 pressure hull
146 acoustic probe
147 sea bed

73 suckers
74 tentacle
75 cuttlefish

76 diving saucer
77 water jet
78 searchlight

79 mechanical arm
80 squid
81 sponge

82 coast guard
83 sand dunes
84 fog signal

17

Food

38	coconuts	104	garlic
39	bananas	105	mint
40	grapes	106	parsley
41	limes	107	rosemary
42	lemons	108	thyme
43	oranges	**109**	**meat**
44	grapefruit	110	ham
45	mangoes	111	bacon
46	paw paws	112	chops
47	figs	113	salami
48	pears	114	steak
49	apples	115	sausages
50	tangerines	**116**	**fish**
51	lychees	117	smoked salmon
52	melons	118	prawns
53	water melons	119	kippers
54	peaches	120	fish cakes
55	plums	121	fish fingers
56	dates	122	sardines
57	apricots	123	tuna fish
58	greengages	124	fish steak
59	redcurrants	125	fish fillet
60	blueberries	126	brown bread
61	strawberries	127	white bread
62	raspberries	128	croissants
63	gooseberries	129	bread rolls
64	cranberries	130	muffins
65	blackberries	131	doughnuts
66	salad	132	breadsticks
67	stew	133	icing
68	spaghetti	134	cake
69	syrup	135	biscuits
70	meat pie	136	French loaf
71	rice	137	scones
72	dumplings	138	pitta bread
73	soup	139	dried beans
74	omelette	140	hot chocolate
75	fried eggs	141	beer
76	hamburger	142	wine
77	pancakes	143	coffee
78	potato chips	144	coffee beans
79	hot dogs	145	tea
80	roast turkey	146	teabag
81	stuffing	147	fruit juice
82	sandwiches	148	milkshake
83	pizza	149	cream
84	quiche	150	sugar
85	caviar	151	jam
86	ice cream	152	flour
87	pâté	153	mustard
88	chocolate sauce	154	salt
89	soufflé	155	pepper
90	jelly	156	honey
91	mousse	157	mayonnaise
92	shish kebabs	158	tomato ketchup
93	éclairs	159	cereal
94	fruit salad	160	nuts
95	cheesecake	161	peanut butter
96	custard	162	sweets
97	pastry	163	gherkins
98	meringues	164	baked beans
99	fruit tart	165	cheese
100	trifle	166	butter
101	**herbs**	167	yoghurt
102	basil	168	marmalade
103	chives	169	raisins

1 vegetables
2 spinach
3 peas
4 carrots
5 potatoes
6 marrow
7 turnip
8 parsnip
9 aubergines
10 courgettes
11 Brussels sprouts
12 leeks
13 broccoli
14 cauliflower
15 celery
16 beans
17 cabbage
18 red cabbage
19 pumpkin
20 onions
21 mushrooms
22 artichokes
23 asparagus
24 beetroot
25 sweetcorn
26 fennel
27 lettuce
28 radishes
29 chicory
30 tomatoes
31 cucumber
32 rhubarb
33 red pepper
34 green pepper
35 avocados
36 fruit
37 pineapple

The castle

1 foot soldier
2 bill
3 kettle hat
4 pike
5 crossbow
6 stirrup
7 quarrel
8 trigger
9 quiver
10 arrows
11 longbow
12 axe
13 flail
14 mace
15 dagger
16 siege tower
17 battering ram
18 ballista
19 sling
20 trebuchet
21 mantlet
22 archer
23 mangonel
24 firepot
25 boiling oil
26 cannon
27 breech
28 touch hole
29 rope wad
30 cannon balls
31 gunpowder
    cartridge
32 muzzle
33 gun carriage
34 taper
35 rammer
36 knight
37 quilted vest
38 squire
39 leggings
40 hood
41 chain mail
42 scale armour
43 plate armour
44 basinet
45 breast plate
46 sabaton
47 roundel
48 tunic
49 great helm
50 coat-of-arms
51 sheath
52 broadsword
53 shin guard
54 lance
55 shield
56 jousting
   tournament
57 quintain
58 plume
59 pavilion
60 nobles

61 coronel
62 horse armour
63 tilt
64 pommel
   saddle
65 crest
66 trumpeters
67 herald
68 castle
69 turret
70 battlements
71 solar
72 keep
73 lancet window
74 baron
75 tailor
76 baroness
77 maid
78 tapestry
79 chaplain
80 cross
81 chapel
82 troubadour
83 pallet
84 gallery
85 minstrel
86 tub
87 candle
88 great hall
89 fireplace
90 spiral staircase
91 barrel
92 dungeon
93 prisoner
94 ball and chain
95 jailer
96 garderobe
97 bench
98 trestle table
99 jester
100 buttress
101 cauldron
102 kitchen shed
103 thatch
104 herb bed
105 walled garden
106 fruit tree
107 bellows
108 great oven
109 spit
110 guard
111 firescreen
112 bakehouse
113 packhorse
114 merchant
115 wooden stairs
116 inner bailey
117 stairwell
118 arrow slit
119 smoke hole
120 smithy
121 armourer

122 peasant
123 fish pond
124 laundress
125 shoemaker
126 woodcutter
127 thatcher
128 outer bailey
129 steward
130 nun
131 monk
132 arch
133 logs

134 hounds
135 keeper-of-the-
   hounds
136 cart
137 hut
138 well
139 dovecote
140 doves
141 stable boy
142 perch
143 falconer
144 falcon

145 falcons' mews
146 wall walk
147 curtain wall
148 sentry
149 merlon
150 crenel
151 hoarding
152 gatehouse
153 portcullis
154 drawbridge
155 beggars
156 ditch

Music

1 bass drum
2 drumsticks
3 snare drum
4 trombone
5 slide
6 water key
7 kettle drum
8 drumhead
9 foot pedal
10 bassoon
11 crook
12 oboe
13 keys
14 reed
15 flute
16 blow-hole
17 violin
18 chin rest
19 violin bow
20 clarinet
21 viola
22 tailpiece
23 scroll
24 tuba
25 valve
26 mouthpiece
27 French horn
28 cor anglais
29 piccolo
30 lip plate
31 cello
32 orchestra
33 tubular bells
34 xylophone
35 organ
36 stops
37 organ pipes
38 percussion
39 cymbals
40 flautist
41 woodwind
42 brass section
43 string section
44 harpist
45 harp
46 violinists
47 viola players
48 music stand
49 conductor
50 sheet music
51 rostrum
52 cellists
53 double bass
   players
54 rock group
55 speaker
56 drumkit
57 floor tom
58 drummer
59 tom toms
60 crash and ride
   cymbal

61 hihat
62 backup singers
63 microphone
64 reed switch
65 amplifier
66 bass guitarist

67 electric piano
68 moog
   syntheziser
69 lead guitarist
70 electric organ
71 electric guitar

72 headstock
73 neck
74 frets
75 pickup
76 scratchplate
77 tremolo arm

78 controls
79 jack plug socket
80 double bass
   bow
81 double bass
82 strings

111 sleigh bells
112 recorder
113 castanets
114 accordion
115 keyboard
116 harmonica
117 jazz band
118 banjo
119 saxophone
120 jazz singer
121 trumpet
122 trumpeter
123 pianist
124 piano
125 metronome
126 pendulum
127 folk singer
128 Spanish guitar
129 soundhole
130 soundboard
131 concertina
132 brass band
133 drum majorette
134 bugle
135 cornet
136 discothèque
137 disc jockey
138 disco dancers
139 dance floor
140 turntable
141 records
142 steel band
143 steel drum
144 cello pan
145 bass pan
146 ping pongs
147 guitar pan
148 conga drum
149 rhythm section
150 bongo drums
151 tambourine
152 jingles
153 cabasas
154 maracas
155 cow bell
156 claves
157 guiro

83 bridge
84 fingerboard
85 tuning pegs
86 glockenspiel
87 dulcimer
88 ukelele
89 mandolin

90 bagpipes
91 melody pipe
92 windbag
93 blowpipe
94 drone pipe
95 tenor drones
96 wood block

97 rattle
98 gong
99 vibraphone
100 koto
101 triangle
102 tambura
103 sitar

104 gourd
105 zither
106 marimba
107 balalaika
108 lute
109 pegbox
110 handbell

In the country

1 otter
2 hedgehog
3 slug
4 shrew
5 stag
6 antlers
7 beetle
8 fawn
9 doe
10 pine cone
11 squirrel
12 drey
13 fox cubs
14 fox
15 badger
16 harvest mouse
17 water vole
18 cloud
19 hang glider
20 hot-air balloon
21 gas burner
22 basket
23 sand bag
24 rainbow
25 windmill
26 rain

27 valley
28 rucksack
29 piton
30 karabiner
31 climbing
   helmet
32 climbing boot
33 rock climber

34 piton hammer
35 cliff
36 climbing rope
37 climbing
   harness
38 village
39 cemetery
40 kite

41 spire
42 tunnel
43 canal
44 barge
45 church
46 telegraph pole
47 garden shed
48 greenhouse

49 creeper
50 house
51 swing
52 garden
53 plant
54 flower bed
55 lawn
56 sand pit

24

72 swallow
73 tortoise
74 pigeon
75 ladybird
76 pheasant
77 grasshopper
78 frog
79 water lily
80 lily pad
81 ant
82 toad
83 bumblebee
84 flower
85 swan
86 caterpillar
87 wasp
88 spider
89 web
90 snail

91 sky
92 hawk
93 hill
94 branch
95 bird
96 nestlings
97 nest
98 quarry
99 power line
100 pylon
101 log cabin
102 lock
103 lake
104 power station
105 hedgerow
106 pony trekker
107 tree
108 forest
109 forester
110 hammock
111 tow bar
112 bridge
113 river bank
114 bush
115 camp site
116 barbecue
117 firewood
118 charcoal
119 picnic table
120 camp bed
121 bark
122 angler
123 river
124 compass
125 birdwatcher
126 binoculars
127 map
128 camping stove
129 guy rope
130 water carrier
131 fly sheet
132 torch
133 tent pole
134 ice box
135 air mattress
136 sleeping bag
137 gas lamp
138 tent
139 tent peg
140 moth
141 roots
142 moss
143 tree stump
144 toadstools

57 paddling pool
58 slide
59 climbing frame
60 butterfly
61 mole hill
62 mole
63 waterfall
64 hiker

65 dragonfly
66 signpost
67 path
68 tackle box
69 fishing rod
70 fishing net
71 grass
72 swallow

73 tortoise
74 pigeon
75 ladybird
76 pheasant
77 grasshopper
78 frog
79 water lily
80 lily pad

81 ant
82 toad
83 bumblebee
84 flower
85 swan
86 caterpillar
87 wasp
88 spider

On the road

1 tandem
2 tricycle
3 scrambler bike
4 racing bike
5 motor scooter
6 moped
7 go-kart
8 bicycle
9 hand grip
10 gear change
   lever
11 handlebar
12 gear cable
13 bell
14 carrier
15 saddle bag
16 saddle
17 seat stem
18 brake lever
19 brake cable
20 horn
21 bicycle lamp
22 bicycle lock
23 rear reflector
24 rear lamp
25 dynamo
26 sprocket
27 chain guard
28 bicycle pump
29 water bottle
   carrier
30 brake calliper
31 mudguard
32 brake block
33 front wheel
34 panniers
35 rear wheel
36 bicycle chain
37 pedal
38 pedal crank
39 kickstand
40 chain wheel
41 frame
42 front fork
43 wheel rim
44 valve
45 spokes
46 spoke reflector
47 inner tube
48 puncture repair
   kit
49 water bottle
50 spanners
51 tyre levers
52 motorbike
53 twist throttle
54 clutch lever
55 rearview mirror
56 pillion seat
57 petrol tank
58 sparking plug
59 carburettor

60 kick start lever
61 rear drum brake
62 front disc brake
63 hydraulic fork
64 rear brake pedal
65 foot rest
66 muffler
67 gauntlets
68 visor
69 crash helmet
70 sports car
71 racing car
72 dragster
73 sidecar
74 beachbuggy
75 vintage car
76 landrover
77 van
78 breakdown
   lorry
79 petrol tanker
80 removal van
81 caravan
82 car transporter
83 coach
84 bus
85 double-decker
   bus
86 trolley bus
87 estate car
88 ambulance
89 fire engine
90 dustcart

91 juggernaut
92 truck
93 garage
94 petrol pump
95 car wash
96 inspection bay
97 roof rack
98 mechanic

99 hydraulic lift
100 air pump
101 car
102 front wing
103 side light
104 front bumper
105 headlamp
106 car radiator

107 fan belt
108 cooling fan
109 cylinder head
110 air filter
111 car battery
112 wing mirror
113 front
    suspension

114 chassis	122 steering wheel	130 gear stick	138 spare wheel	146 petrol cap
115 piston	123 dashboard	131 hand brake	139 reversing light	147 wheel hub
116 distributor	124 seat belt	132 back seat	140 foot pump	148 wedge
117 oil filter	125 headrest	133 silencer	141 number plate	149 oil can
118 sump	126 accelerator	134 universal joint	142 exhaust pipe	150 tool box
119 speedometer	127 foot brake	135 drive shaft	143 rear bumper	151 spider spanner
120 petrol gauge	128 clutch	136 boot	144 rear light	152 jack
121 windscreen	129 gear box	137 brake light	145 indicator light	153 tyre

In the city

1 skyscraper
2 flats
3 balcony
4 fire station
5 siren
6 service station
7 flyover
8 fire escape
9 hotel
10 walkway
11 bellboy
12 doorman
13 suitcase
14 reception
15 lobby
16 delivery van
17 office building
18 switchboard
19 typist
20 office
21 mural
22 skylight
23 post office
24 sorting office
25 letterbox
26 postman
27 parcels
28 mail van
29 café
30 waitress
31 awning
32 statue
33 crowd
34 barrier
35 bank
36 bank teller
37 security guard
38 security van
39 roof terrace
40 bank vault
41 supermarket
42 storeroom
43 neon sign
44 trolley
45 queue
46 cinema
47 shop sign
48 fish shop
49 fishmonger
50 shop assistant
51 chemist
52 cash register
53 newspaper
54 newspaper
   stand
55 pillar
56 street sign
57 hairdryer
58 hairdressing salon
59 hairdresser
60 road sign
61 policeman

62 cyclist
63 telephone kiosk
64 telephone cable
65 steps

66 woman
67 gas pipe
68 flag
69 flagpole

70 taxi rank
71 window cleaner
72 department
   store

28

73 street lamp
74 hospital
75 school
76 school teacher
77 school children
78 taxi
79 road sweeper
80 rubbish cart
81 litter
82 revolving door
83 window dresser
84 dummy
85 porter
86 patient
87 ramp
88 pushchair
89 traffic warden
90 parking meter
91 park bench
92 nanny
93 pram
94 fountain
95 park
96 gatepost
97 railings
98 motor cyclist
99 pillion rider
100 bus stop
101 bus driver
102 passengers
103 smoke
104 fireman
105 warning light
106 fire
107 fire hose
108 jumping sheet
109 advertisement
110 bookstall
111 bookseller
112 carrier bag
113 shoe stall
114 shoes
115 souvenir stall
116 tee shirts
117 poster
118 badges
119 fruit stall
120 stretcher
121 accident
122 fire hydrant
123 pavement
124 kerbstone
125 tramp
126 paintings
127 traffic light
128 vegetable stall
129 toy stall
130 clothes stall
131 jersey
132 trousers
133 dresses
134 hats
135 clothes rack
136 socks
137 coats
138 flower seller
139 street map
140 transformer
141 manhole cover
142 litter bin
143 crossing
144 pedestrian
145 manhole
146 electricity cable
147 man
148 underpass
149 water pipe
150 sewage
151 sewer
152 valve box
153 gate key
154 grating

29

Toys and games

1 doll
2 rag doll
3 princess
4 prince
5 king
6 crown
7 queen
8 fairy
9 wand
10 ballerina
11 broomstick
12 witch
13 bride
14 bridegroom
15 bridesmaid
16 page
17 sailor
18 mobile
19 parrot
20 blackboard
21 pencil case
22 fountain pen
23 ballpoint pen
24 pencils
25 wax crayons
26 rubber
27 ruler
28 poster paints
29 felt tip pens
30 numbers
31 letters
32 notebook
33 abacus
34 beads
35 building blocks
36 magnet
37 globe
38 chemistry set
39 test tube
40 spirit burner
41 beaker
42 funnel
43 flask
44 magnifying glass
45 microscope
46 kaleidoscope
47 balloons
48 paper hats
49 fireworks
50 lantern
51 totem pole
52 wigwam
53 head-dress
54 Indian chief
55 squaw
56 papoose
57 fort
58 cavalry man
59 Indian brave
60 tomahawk
61 jack-in-the-box
62 music box

63 money box
64 ferris wheel
65 roundabout
66 rocking horse
67 puppet theatre

68 string puppet
69 glove puppet
70 dolls' house
71 cradle
72 polar bear

73 panda
74 rhinoceros
75 camel
76 penguins
77 kangaroo

78 zebra
79 leopard
80 monkey
81 crocodile
82 ghost

83 angel
84 wizard
85 pistol
86 pirate
87 treasure

88 monster
89 dragon
90 elf
91 gnome
92 sleigh

93 Father Christmas
94 teddy bear
95 reindeer
96 Christmas
   stocking

97 purse
98 money
99 embroidery
100 wool
101 knitting needle
102 tank
103 infantry men
104 crane
105 excavator
106 remote control
    car
107 race track
108 spaceship
109 hobby horse
110 pogo stick
111 stilts
112 hulahoop
113 scooter
114 skipping rope
115 spinning top
116 skittles
117 marbles
118 board game
119 playing cards
120 dice
121 counters
122 chess board
123 chessmen
124 jigsaw puzzle
125 dominoes
126 puzzle
127 snooker table
128 snooker ball
129 cue
130 robot
131 rattle
132 lunch box
133 penknife
134 key ring
135 keys
136 torch
137 typewriter
138 radio
139 record player
140 walkie-talkie
141 cassette
    recorder
142 cassettes
143 electronic
    games
144 cartridge
145 television game
146 handsets
147 computer
148 calculator
149 tiger
150 lion
151 elephant
152 hippopotamus
153 koala bear
154 giraffe
155 ostrich
156 buffalo
157 wolf
158 snake
159 dinosaur

Jobs people do

1 **weaver**
2 dye bath
3 loom
4 woven cloth
5 cloth roller
6 ratchet
7 treadles
8 yarn
9 boat shuttle
10 rug beater
11 bobbin winder
12 **potter**
13 kiln
14 clay
15 modelling tools
16 callipers
17 potter's knife
18 turning tool
19 cutting wire
20 potter's wheel
21 splashpan
22 glaze
23 **blacksmith**
24 fuller
25 flatter
26 stamp
27 scroll iron
28 scroll dog
29 vice
30 fire irons
31 firehood
32 iron
33 water trough
34 tongs
35 swage block
36 horseshoeing
    box
37 mandrel
38 sledge hammer
39 anvil
40 **artist**
41 canvas
42 model
43 canvas
    stretcher
44 paintbox
45 oil paints
46 smock
47 rag
48 easel
49 sketch pad
50 dais
51 stapler
52 palette
53 dipper
54 palette knife
55 brushes
56 painting knife
57 charcoal sticks
58 turpentine
59 **gardener**
60 compost heap

61 trellis
62 cloche
63 flowerpots
64 cold frame
65 twine
66 dibber

67 gardening
    gloves
68 garden tools
69 wheelbarrow
70 shears
71 lawn mower

72 trug
73 seedlings
74 seed tray
75 watering can
76 rose
77 bulbs

78 secateurs
79 **dressmaker**
80 sewing
    machine
81 cotton reel
82 tension dial

32

106 mitre block
107 moulding
108 photographer
109 camera
110 wind-on lever
111 shutter button
112 shutter speed
control
113 flash shoe
114 rewind lever
115 aperture
control
116 focus control
117 lens
118 light screen
119 wind machine
120 film cassette
121 tripod
122 background
paper
123 darkroom
124 safelight
125 umbrella light
126 strobe light
127 power unit
128 telephoto lens
129 slide projector
130 flash gun
131 camera case
132 prints
133 cook
134 sieve
135 whisk
136 rolling pin
137 apron
138 piping bag
139 spatula
140 pastry brush
141 cake tin
142 chopping board
143 cook's knife
144 lemon squeezer
145 scales
146 measuring jug
147 food processor
148 wooden spoons
149 mixing bowl
150 grater
151 silversmith
152 silver
153 bench block
154 burnisher
155 propane torch
156 stones
157 bracelets
158 polishing
machine
159 jeweller's saw
160 tweezers
161 pliers
162 brooch
163 ring
164 necklace

83 pressure foot
84 bobbin
85 tape measure
86 scissors
87 needles
88 material

89 sewing box
90 dress pattern
91 buttons
92 pins
93 pin cushion
94 thread

95 picture framer
96 hardboard
97 picture glass
98 mounting
board
99 metal ruler

100 G-cramp
101 hand drill
102 mitre cramp
103 claw hammer
104 craft knife
105 tenon saw

33

On the rails

1 **marshalling yard**
2 freight train
3 freight wagon
4 scanner
5 container
6 grab
7 gantry crane
8 boxcar
9 lighting tower
10 open goods wagon
11 signal box
12 signalman
13 tank wagon
14 warehouse
15 flat wagon
16 loading foreman
17 weighing machine
18 crates
19 shunting signal
20 signals
21 shunting engine
22 **station**
23 station clock
24 loudspeaker
25 left luggage office
26 ticket office
27 information office
28 newsagent
29 magazines
30 water fountain
31 underground entrance
32 thief
33 handbag
34 platform number
35 walking-stick
36 electric truck
37 ticket machine
38 turnstile
39 fire extinguisher
40 lift
41 emergency button
42 landing
43 escalator
44 emergency stairs
45 street musician
46 ventilation shaft
47 steel girder
48 fan
49 underground train map
50 exit sign

51 vending machine
52 electric rail
53 underground train
54 platform

55 mailbags
56 buffer
57 railway track
58 **electric locomotive**

59 engineer
60 insulator
61 roof cable
62 oil cooler
63 battery box

64 electric motor
65 pantograph
66 overhead wire
67 windscreen wiper

86 radiator fan
87 warning horns
88 passenger train
89 sleeping compartment
90 foldaway bunk
91 dining car
92 menu
93 waiter
94 barman
95 bottles
96 toilet
97 connecting corridor
98 passenger car
99 briefcase
100 luggage rack
101 seat
102 armrest
103 ticket collector
104 forklift truck
105 barrow
106 luggage
107 cafeteria
108 self-service counter
109 photograph booth
110 train guard
111 waiting room
112 timetable
113 railway map
114 steam engine
115 smokebox door
116 hinge
117 smokestack
118 blast pipe
119 smokebox
120 boiler
121 steam dome
122 water feed
123 fire tubes
124 fire box
125 safety valves
126 whistle lever
127 regulator
128 reversing lever
129 driver's cab
130 train driver
131 driver's seat
132 tender
133 coal
134 water tank
135 brake hose
136 leading wheel
137 cylinder
138 sand pipe
139 piston rod
140 crosshead
141 connecting rod
142 crank
143 coupling rod
144 driving wheel
145 ashpan
146 grate
147 axle bearing

68 control switches	71 front coupling	76 spike	81 generator
69 dead man's handle	72 sleeper	77 baseplate	82 bogie
70 handwheel	73 ballast	78 T-rail	83 wheel tapper
	74 rail	**79 diesel lomotive**	84 diesel engine
	75 fishplate	80 radio telephone	85 cooling unit

In the studio

1 actress
2 actor
3 producer
4 script
5 writer
6 casting director
7 clipboard
8 filing cabinet
9 tape recorder
10 paint trolley
11 scenic artist
12 scenery
13 backdrop
14 floor plan
15 desk lamp
16 set designer
17 scenery builder
18 drawing board
19 set model
20 prop store
21 skeleton
22 prop master
23 crutch
24 masks
25 wheelchair
26 throne
27 artificial plant
28 trophy
29 gramophone
30 costume room
31 caps
32 bonnet
33 cloak
34 top hat
35 shawl
36 veil
37 coat hanger
38 tutu
39 historical costume
40 bouquet
41 costume designer
42 wedding dress
43 belt
44 raincoat
45 sleeve
46 collar
47 medals
48 uniform
49 ties
50 blouses
51 spectacles
52 wigs
53 mirror lights
54 stethoscope
55 waistcoat
56 make-up artist
57 hair curlers
58 moustaches
59 scar
60 blow dryer

61 cotton wool
62 plasticine
63 false beard
64 false nose
65 grease paint

66 false teeth
67 make-up box
68 lipstick
69 face powder
70 powder puff

71 headphones
72 teleprompt operator
73 teleprompt
74 weather reporter

36

75 weather chart	80 newscaster
76 caption roller	81 **studio**
77 digital clock	82 overhead light
78 desk	83 spotlight
79 earpiece	84 scarf

85 cleaner	90 nurse
86 mop	91 syringe
87 curtain screen	92 thermometer
88 dressing gown	93 doctor
89 medicine bottle	94 calendar

95 drip
96 plaster cast
97 present
98 visitor
99 weight
100 scene shifter
101 call boy
102 bandage
103 sticking plaster
104 pills
105 boom operator
106 boom
107 microphone
108 temperature chart
109 studio camera
110 sound technician
111 cameraman
112 floor manager
113 video tape
    recorder
114 studio monitor
115 crane camera
116 zoom lens
117 cue card
118 viewfinder
119 focusing handle
120 pedestal
121 camera cable
122 sound control
    room
123 sound
    supervisor
124 sound engineer
125 production
    control room
126 vision mixer
127 director
128 monitor screen
129 stop watch
130 production
    assistant
131 technical
    manager
132 vision control
    room
133 vision controller
134 lighting director
135 film camera
136 clapperboard
137 stetson
138 sheriff
139 holster
140 spurs
141 chaps
142 bullets
143 handcuffs
144 gun
145 lasso
146 film set
147 sound recordist
148 cowboy
149 bandit
150 stagecoach
151 stuntman
152 money bag
153 airbag

On the water

1 **ocean liner**
2 lido
3 sports deck
4 florist's
5 shopping arcade
6 sun deck
7 exhaust stack
8 smoke deflector
9 nightclub
10 lookout tower
11 navigation bridge and chartroom
12 crew's quarters
13 car lift
14 cabins
15 single berth cabin
16 staterooms
17 cocktail lounge
18 library
19 theatre and lecture hall
20 casino
21 beauty salon
22 laundry room
23 ballroom
24 wine cellar
25 restaurant
26 children's playroom
27 portholes
28 bow thrusters
29 hawsehole
30 **hovercraft**
31 control deck
32 car ramp

71 flare
72 sextant
73 life buoy
74 batten
75 sail bag
76 anemometer
77 barometer
78 chart
79 paddle
80 fender
81 pennant
82 bailer
83 launching trolley
84 **cargo ship**
85 poop deck
86 davit
87 lifeboats
88 funnel
89 fog horn
90 wheelhouse
91 cross-trees
92 crow's nest
93 foredeck
94 derrick
95 forecastle
96 windlass
97 jack
98 jackstaff
99 hull
100 propeller shaft
101 turbines
102 engine room
103 anchor cable
104 **tanker**
105 fire tower
106 mooring winch
107 kingpost
108 cargo tanks
109 **rescue launch**
110 guard rail
111 inflatable liferaft
112 towing davit

38

33 flexible skirt	40 powerboat	48 bow fender	56 trawl net	63 catamaran
34 passenger	41 fireboat	49 pilot house	57 bucket dredger	64 trimaran
steps	42 hosereels	50 searchlight	58 bucket chain	65 outrigger
35 hydrofoil	43 scuppers	51 towing lights	59 chute	66 schooner
36 motor boat	44 police launch	52 tow hook	60 sloop	67 foresail
37 deckhouse	45 lightship	53 capstan	61 spinnaker	68 racing yacht
38 outboard motor	46 lantern mast	54 trawler	62 spinnaker	69 genoa
39 steering arm	**47 tug**	55 trawl gallows	boom	70 keel

113 aircraft carrier	121 car ferry	**130 sailing dinghy**	139 bow	148 halyard
114 arrester wire	122 car deck	131 helmsman	140 stern	149 rudder blade
115 hangar deck	123 hinged bow	132 crew	141 traveller	150 drain hole
116 launching	124 dhow	133 port side	142 buoyancy tank	151 starboard side
catapult	125 gondola	134 stay	143 transom	152 main sheet
117 aircraft lift	126 rowing boat	135 mast	144 tiller	153 thwart
118 jets (fighter)	127 rowlock	136 mainsail	145 toe strap	154 kicking strap
119 crash barrier	128 punt	137 batten pocket	146 jib sheet	155 boom
120 safety net	129 junk	138 jib	147 centreboard	156 block

In space

1 lightning rod
2 radio telescope
3 gantry
4 space launch
   station
5 launch pad
6 space rocket
7 rocket engines
8 retro-rockets
9 first stage
10 second stage
11 liquid oxygen
   tank
12 third stage
13 instrument unit
14 lunar module
   hangar
15 engine nozzle
16 service module
17 launch escape
   tower
**18 command
   module**
19 recovery
   beacon
20 docking probe
21 main recovery
   parachute
22 crew
   compartment
23 yaw thrusters
24 heatshield
25 roll thrusters
26 padded couch
27 pitch thrusters
28 hatch door
29 rendezvous
   window
30 weather
   satellite
31 communications
   satellite
32 earth resources
   satellite
33 space probe
34 cosmic ray
   detector
35 space station
36 solar shield
37 solar panel
38 micrometeoroid
   shield
39 orbital
   workshop
40 sleep
   compartment

41 exercise bicycle
42 solar wing
43 deployment
   boom
44 docking port
45 lunar module

46 docking hatch
47 rendezvous
   radar antenna
48 inflight antenna
49 tracking light
50 entry hatch

51 exhaust
   deflector
52 ascent engine
53 entry/exit
   platform
54 landing gear

55 descent engine
56 thermal
   insulation
57 foot pad
58 moon rock
59 lunar surface

60 lunar rover
61 high-gain
   antenna
62 low-gain antenna
63 camera pack
64 display console

84 penlight pocket
85 chronograph
86 extra-vehicular glove
87 checklist
88 utility pocket
89 rubber innersuit
90 lunar overshoe
91 clip
92 moonwalk
93 space shuttle
94 nose cap
95 heat insulation tiles
96 rocket thrusters
97 oxidizer tank
98 pilot's seat
99 docking controls
100 commander's seat
101 rearview window
102 access tunnel
103 payload bay
104 payload bay door
105 space radiator
106 payload specialists
107 space laboratory
108 robot arm
109 space telescope
110 pallet
111 main wheels
112 delta wing
113 elevon
114 magnetometer
115 sensor
116 umbilical line
117 spacewalk
118 speed brake
119 manoeuvring engine
120 launch support
121 solid rocket booster
122 external tank
123 drogue parachute
124 comet
125 meteorite
126 star
127 Milky Way
128 planet
129 solar system
130 sunspot
131 Sun
132 solar flare
133 Mercury
134 Venus
135 Mars
136 Earth
137 asteroids
138 Jupiter
139 Saturn's rings
140 Saturn
141 Moon
142 Uranus
143 Neptune
144 Pluto

65 television camera
66 wiremesh wheel
67 dust guard
68 sample bag dispenser
69 rock tongs
70 underseat bag stowage
71 tool carrier
72 scoop
73 footprint
74 moon dust
75 moon crater
76 astronaut
77 sunglasses pocket
78 transceiver
79 airtank
80 portable life support system
81 pressurized helmet
82 spacesuit
83 control box

41

Index

blind **72**, p.6
blinker **63**, p.10
block **156**, p.39
blouses **50**, p.36
blow dryer **60**, p.36
blow-hole **16**, p.22
blow lamp **82**, p.4
blowpipe **93**, p.23
blueberries **60**, p.18
boar **34**, p.12
board game **118**, p.31
boarding pass **107**, p.14
boat house **152**, p.11
boat shuttle **9** p.32
bobbin **84**, p.33
bobbin winder **11**, p.32
bobsleigh racing 80, p.11
bogie **82**, p.34
boiler **120**, p.35
boiling oil **25**, p.21
bollard **10**, p.16
bolster chisel **66**, p.4
bone **65**, p.6
bongo drums **150**, p.23
bonnet **32**, p.36
bookcase **104**, p.7
bookseller **111**, p.29
bookstall **110**, p.29
boom **106**, p.37
boom **155**, p.39
boom operator **105**, p.37
boost gauge **6**, p.14
boot (car) **136**, p.27
boots **60**, p.12
bottles **95**, p.35
boule **107**, p.11
boules 106, p.11
bouquet **40**, p.36
bow **139**, p.39
bow (archery) **117**, p.11
bow fender **48**, p.38
bowl **95**, p.11
bowler **30**, p.10
bowling crease **32**, p.10
bowling green **94**, p.11
bowling mat **93**, p.11
bowls 92, p.11
bowman **67**, p.10
bowstring **116**, p.11
bow thrusters **28**, p.38
boxcar **8**, p.34
boxer **53**, p.8
boxes **4**, p.6
boxing 51, p.8
boxing ring **55**, p.8
brace and bit **149**, p.5
bracelets **157**, p.33
brake block **32**, p.26
brake cable **19**, p.26
brake calliper **30**, p.26
brake hose **135**, p.35
brake lever **18**, p.26

brake light **137**, p.27
brakeman **82**, p.11
branch **94**, p.25
brass band 132, p.23
brass section **42**, p.22
bread board **89**, p.6
bread rolls **129**, p.19
breadsticks **132**, p.19
breakdown lorry **78**, p.27
breakwater **95**, p.17
breast plate **45**, p.20
breech **27**, p.21
breeches **71**, p.8
breeze block **54**, p.4
brick hammer **71**, p.4
bricklayer **62**, p.4
bricks **48**, p.4
bride **13**, p.30
bridegroom **14**, p.30
bridesmaid **15**, p.30
bridge **112**, p.25
bridge (on double bass)
   83, p.23
briefcase **99**, p.35
broadsword **52**, p.20
broccoli **13**, p.18
brooch **162**, p.33
broomstick **11**, p.30
brown bread **126**, p.19
brushes **55**, p.32
Brussels sprouts **11**, p.18
buck **85**, p.9
bucket **32**, p.16
bucket chain **58**, p.38
bucket dredger **57**, p.38
buffalo **156**, p.31
buffer **56**, p.34
bugle **134**, p.23
building blocks **35**, p.30
bulb (light) **10**, p.6
bulbs (garden) **77**, p.32
bulkhead **70**, p.15
bull **29**, p.12
bulldozer **1**, p.4
bullets **142**, p.37
bull's eye **121**, p.11
bumblebee **83**, p.25
bunkbeds **57**, p.7
bunker **112**, p.9
buoy **98**, p.17
buoyancy tank **142**, p.39
burglar alarm **92**, p.5
burnisher **154**, p.33
bus **84**, p.27
bus driver **101**, p.29
bush **114**, p.25
bus stop **100**, p.29
butter **166**, p.19
butter dish **138**, p.6
butterfly **60**, p.24
buttons **91**, p.33
buttress **100**, p.21

Cc

cabasas **153**, p.23
cabbage **17**, p.18
cabins **14**, p.38
cable **131**, p.17
cable car **4**, p.10
caddie **106**, p.9
café **29**, p.28
cafeteria **107**, p.35
cage **130**, p.17
cake **134**, p.19
cake tin **141**, p.33
calculator **148**, p.31
calendar **94**, p.37
calf **27**, p.12
call boy **101**, p.37
callipers **16**, p.32
camel **75**, p.30
camera 109, p.33
camera cable **121**, p.37
camera case **131**, p.33
cameraman **111**, p.37
camera pack **63**, p.41
camp bed **120**, p.25
camping stove **128**, p.25
camp site **115**, p.25
canal **43**, p.24
candle **87**, p.21
candlestick **156**, p.7
cannon 26, p.21
cannon balls **30**, p.21
canoeing 65, p.10
canvas **41**, p.32
canvas stretcher **43**, p.32
caps **31**, p.36
capstan **53**, p.38
captain **83**, p.11
caption roller **76**, p.36
car 101, p.27
caravan **81**, p.27
car battery **111**, p.27
carburettor **59**, p.26
car deck **122**, p.39
car ferry **121**, p.39
cargo container **58**, p.14
cargo hold **67**, p.14
cargo ship 84, p.39
cargo tanks **108**, p.39
car hire **116**, p.15
car lift **13**, p.38
car park **49**, p.14
carpenter **136**, p.5
carpet layer **93**, p.5
car radiator **106**, p.27

car ramp **32**, p.38
carrier **14**, p.26
carrier bag **112**, p.29
carrots **4**, p.18
cart **136**, p.21
carthorse **85**, p.13
car transporter **82**, p.27
cartridge **144**, p.31
cartridges (rifle) **104**, p.11
carving fork **147**, p.7
carving knife **146**, p.7
car wash **95**, p.27
cash register **52**, p.28
casino **20**, p.38
casserole dish **152**, p.7
cassette recorder **141**, p.31
cassettes **142**, p.31
castanets **113**, p.23
casting director **6**, p.36
castle 68, p.20
cat **56**, p.12
catamaran **63**, p.38
catcher **42**, p.10
caterpillar **86**, p.25
cat flap **64**, p.6
cattle grid **104**, p.13
cauldron **101**, p.21
cauliflower **14**, p.18
cavalry man **58**, p.30
cave **1**, p.16
caviar **85**, p.18
cavity wall **43**, p.4
ceiling **101**, p.5
ceiling joist **53**, p.4
celery **15**, p.18
cellist **52**, p.22
cello, **31**, p.22
cello pan **144**, p.23
cement **29**, p.4
cement mixer **28**, p.4
cemetery **39**, p.24
centreboard **147**, p.39
centre line **99**, p.11
cereal **159**, p.19
cesta (basket) **133**, p.11
cinema **46**, p.28
cinema screen **73**, p.15
chain guard **27**, p.26
chain mail **41**, p.20
chain wheel **40**, p.26
chair **94**, p.6
chair lift **5**, p.10
changing room **6**, p.16
chapel **81**, p.21
chaplain **79**, p.21
chaps **141**, p.37
charcoal **118**, p.25
charcoal sticks **57**, p.32
chart **78**, p.39
chassis **114**, p.27
check-in desk **111**, p.14
checklist **87**, p.41

Dd